Curious George

Lost and Found

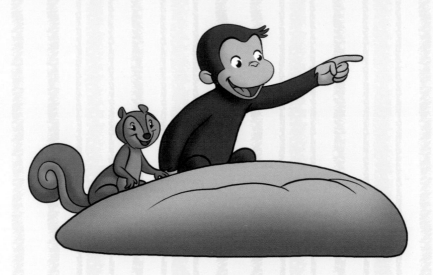

Adaptation by Erica Zappy
Based on the TV series teleplay written by Joe Fallon

Houghton Mifflin Company, Boston 2008

For information about permission to reproduce selections from this book, write to Permissions, Houghton Mifflin Company, 215 Park Avenue South, New York, New York 10003.

Library of Congress Cataloging-in-Publication Data is on file.
ISBN-13: 978-0-618-89197-9

Design by Afsoon Razavi
www.houghtonmifflinbooks.com

Manufactured in Singapore
TWP 10 9 8 7 6 5 4 3 2 1

It was the weekend, and George was excited. He and his friend had left the city for their country house.

After a long drive, George was happy to arrive. He was looking forward to feeding the ducks.

"Don't wander far, George," said the man with the yellow hat as their neighbor Mrs. Renkin drove up to say hello.

But someone else had wandered off — Mrs. Renkin's chicks! George's friend offered to help find them. Meanwhile, George headed toward the river.

At the river, George fed the ducks with his friend Jumpy Squirrel. They found a raft that let them get closer to their duck friends . . .

. . . so close that George felt just like a duck as he floated down the river.
Uh-oh! The raft had drifted away from the shore!

George enjoyed his trip down the river with all of his hungry duck friends.

    But Jumpy was worried. They were lost, just like the chicks.

The raft passed some crooked trees and a big rock that looked like a duck.

The big duck rock made the ducks quack and George smile, but Jumpy was too worried to sightsee. The sun was setting. How were they going to find their way back to the farm?

When they reached a bend in the river, George and Jumpy spotted a silo.

Hooray! It looked like the Renkins' farm!

They waited until the raft neared the shore, then jumped off and headed toward the silo. But it wasn't the right farm. The Renkins' silo was red.

They were still lost. They looked around. Nothing looked familiar. Except . . . THE BIG DUCK ROCK!

It was a landmark. Maybe it would help them find their way home.

George drew a map.
He remembered the big duck rock, the crooked trees, and the silo at the
Renkins' farm. George also remembered that the sun set behind the red silo
every night.

George and Jumpy decided they should follow the sun. It would help them find their way back to the farm, especially if they looked for other landmarks along the way.

As George and Jumpy walked back to the farm, Jumpy bumped into their friends who were lost . . . the chicks!

The chicks did not understand how to use landmarks to navigate, but they were happy to follow the squirrel and monkey back to the farm.

At the farm, Mrs. Renkin and the man with the yellow hat were surprised when George and Jumpy showed up with the chicks in tow.

"George, weren't you supposed to be feeding the ducks?" asked the man with the yellow hat. George tried to explain.

But it was easier to let the chicks do all the squawking!

FIND YOUR WAY

When George got lost, he made a map so he could find his way home. Maps are usually drawn on a flat surface, such as a sheet of paper, and use pictures or symbols to show you where real places are located. You can make a map, too, of your bedroom, your backyard, or even your neighborhood.

To Make a Treasure Map

You will need these things:

- Sheets of paper (white is best)
- Markers or crayons
- A treasure!

1. Pick a secret spot in your backyard and hide something — that's the treasure.

2. Draw the outline of your backyard and then draw the important things that are in it. Here are some examples of landmarks: a swing set, trees, a swimming pool, a garden, a patio, or a shed.

3. Mark the spot where you've hidden the treasure with an "X" on your map, and give the maps to your friends or family. See who can find the treasure first!

BUILD YOUR OWN RAFT

You might not have a raft as big as George's, but you can build your own small raft out of wooden sticks.

You'll need these things:

- Wooden craft sticks
- Glue

1. Line up several sticks vertically on a flat surface.

2. Take one stick and put glue along one side of it. Now place it horizontally across the sticks you lined up, about a quarter inch from their tops.

3. Take another stick with glue along one side and place it across the line of sticks, about a quarter inch from their bottom ends.

4. Let the sticks dry for an hour before putting the raft in water.

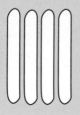  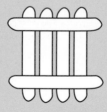

Check with an adult before floating your raft in the sink, bathtub, or kiddie pool. Guess how many pennies you can place on the raft before it sinks. Now test your theory by adding them one at a time.